The Cthulhu Child

David Brian

u   wishes!

David Brian

Night-Flyer

The Cthulhu Child

2013 David Brian

2013 Night-Flyer Publishing

ISBN-13: 978-1497432994
ISBN-10: 1497432995

This edition published in 2014 by Night-Flyer Publishing

The Cthulhu Child

Also by David Brian

Dark Albion

Carmilla: The Wolves of Styria

Carmilla: A Dark Fugue

Kaleen Rae: And Other Weird Tales

This one is for Karen. You brighten my days.

Table of Contents

The Cthulhu Child

Jennifer Bueller was not a woman known for making stupid decisions. Today though, as she gritted her teeth and cursed under her breath, it occurred to her this wasn't turning out to have been one of her better judgment calls.

It had been almost two hours since she and Megan had left Hull, with the intention of being at her sister Cathy's Glasgow home in time for lunch, and the late morning sun was now beating down mercilessly on the windshield of the Corsa. The air-con hadn't worked properly in almost a year, and the temperature inside the car was continuing to climb. As was Megan's temper. These days, the girl was always volatile!

Maybe it was just an age thing, teen hormones playing havoc with female sensitivities? Jennifer had no way of knowing for certain, but she knew that sometimes, her daughter could be a real bitch!

And now, with it looking highly dubious they would even reach Glasgow before late in the afternoon, Jennifer knew the girl would be out to give her a torrid time.

After hearing via the radio that the M6 motorway was closed to all northbound traffic, Jennifer had been faced with the rather unpleasant choice of upsetting her daughter by postponing their trip, or finding an alternative route. But she had promised Megan a day out, and so she had no intention of turning back. Thus, she had taken what was turning out to be the not so clever decision to travel across country through Northumberland. She was now incomprehensibly lost. The Sat-Nav had died over an hour earlier, and for no obvious reason. And now the lack of any workable signal on her cell-phone was aggravating the situation even further.

"Mum, I'm telling you, I need to pee!"

"Oh Megan, sweetheart, can't you wait?"

"Seriously, Mum, you've been telling me to hold it in for the last forty minutes, do you really want me to wet the damn seat? Find somewhere to stop, because you're seriously beginning to do my friggin head in now!"

Jennifer, as was so often the case, chose to ignore her daughter's outburst. Life as a single parent could be tough, and it often made for a far easier life to just let Megan blow off some steam. "Well, it's probably going to be at least that long again before we reach any major A-roads, at least we should find some services there, but on these back roads, I doubt it?"

"Then just pull over and I'll squat in a verge. It's not like there's anyone about for Christ sake!"

"I don't think so, young lady. No daughter of mine is going to expose herself in public!"

"Expose myself in public? Jeez, there's not a soul about, it's like morguesville around here!"

"Morguesville? You know there's no such word, right?"

"Whatever!"

Jennifer once again chose not to respond to the precocious fourteen year olds attitude, although the girl's observation about the bleakness of these roads wasn't completely lost to her. It was a fact that since having passed Haydon Bridge, some thirty minutes earlier, there hadn't been any other traffic on the road journeying in either direction.

The ten year old Corsa in which they were traveling was virtually bomb proof, and had successfully completed the Glasgow trip on eight previous occasions. Its reliability in delivering them safely to their destination was never a doubt in Jennifer's mind, although she was beginning to find it a tad disturbing that she had managed to navigate them quite so far off the beaten track. Nonetheless, she would not turn back, because as was ever the case, Cathy seemed to be the only person on the planet who was able to communicate with Megan. Cathy had a bond with the girl, and it wouldn't have been unfair to say she was the only person Megan showed any respect for. Quite why it should be that the girl was more responsive to her auntie, than to her own mother, was a question which was not lost on Jennifer, and she had spent many long nights lying awake contemplating her own failings.

"There, Mum!" screeched Megan, leaning across from the back seat, and pointing with a sizeable measure of desperation towards the large flashing neon burger, a few hundred meters along the road in front of them.

"They'll have toilets!"

"That's odd," observed Jennifer, somewhat puzzled as to why anyone would choose to open a burger joint along such a remote stretch.

"Stop the car, Mum!"

"I guess we'd better see if they're open. After all, I wouldn't want you sitting in a wet patch, now would I?"

"Ha, bloody ha! Seriously, Mum, you're not funny. And I'm busting for a piddle!"

"Megan Bueller!"

"What?"

"Don't say piddle. It's an awful word!"

"You're so old!"

As Jennifer pulled a hard left, and swung the Corsa onto the gravel lined forecourt of the diner, loose chippings churned up beneath the vehicles tires and rattled noisily against the undercarriage of the car. She pulled to a stop, alongside an outdoor seating area, and looked around.

Set away to the right of them, there was a children's play zone, fitted with climbing frames and slides. Although judging from the state of disrepair on show, it didn't look as though it had been either utilized or maintained in years.

The seated area itself looked truly hideous: Tacky yellow plastic chairs stacked, beside garish purple tables, which in turn were adorned with crimson parasols. Rubbish bins in the shape of burgers had been strategically placed all around the area. Jennifer found it quite amusing that some not so clever soul, had taken the business decision to associate their primary source of retail with waste produce.

The main property was illuminated by a neon burger, decorated with a huge smiling face, proudly flashing the message *'Bertie Burger welcomes you. We are open for business.'* The building was constructed of red brick, although when it was last cleaned Jennifer couldn't say. The outer walls were coated with a grimy residue, such as one finds layering the exterior of properties positioned alongside major through roads, and thus subjected to an almost constant dousing from vehicle emissions. In those circumstances it is usual for discoloration of the stonework to occur, but this place was set well back from a main road. It would have taken sixty years worth of passing traffic to account for the unkempt grubbiness of the brickwork.

To the other side of the main building there was an old Toyota pick-up, parked alongside a smaller red-brick outhouse. The poor state of the vehicle fitted in well with the neglected appearance of the buildings, and this suggested to Jennifer, rightly or wrongly, that the pick-up probably belonged to the proprietor of the burger bar. There was a persistent high-pitched whine being emitted from the smaller brick building, which Jennifer guessed - based on her experience of having once spent five horrible years working within a meat storage plant - probably housed refrigeration units of some description. Looking around, Jennifer wasn't surprised to see that theirs was the only vehicle parked on the forecourt.

"What do you reckon, Mum?"

"What, to this place? Not a lot!"

"Are we going in, because I'm starving?"

"You're always starving! I thought that we stopped because you needed to use the lavatory?"

"I do need the loo, but we might as well grab some scoff while we're here."

"Grab some scoff? I really have done such a wonderful job raising you. I should be so, so proud!"

"Whatever! Can we go? Otherwise I really am going to pee my knickers."

Jennifer glanced at the clock on the dash; it was a few minutes after midday. It was not surprising really that the girl was starting to get hungry, at the rate they were going it would be teatime before they reached Glasgow. She was a little peckish herself, but she really didn't fancy eating at a dump like this.

As she unclipped her seatbelt and opened the driver's door, Jennifer had the strangest feeling of being watched. Straightening herself up to her best height as she exited the car, she looked first towards the burger joint and then all around; scanning the farthest reaches of the gravel lined forecourt and on to a small copse beyond. There was no one in view; in fact the whole area was almost deathly still, with not even the sight of an overhead bird to adorn the panorama. The slight north-westerly breeze bore the aroma of griddled burgers and onions across the courtyard, carried on a nostril thickened scent of deep-fat frying oil. It occurred to Jennifer that someone obviously chose to partake of dining within the premises. Otherwise, in these hard times of struggling economic crisis, the place would have surely closed down long ago.

"Are we going in then, or what?"

Megan's question distracted Jennifer from whatever thing it was, that was beginning to nag away in the back of her mind.

"Come on then, kiddo, let's go find the toilets."

"Kiddo? You do realize I'm fourteen, right?"

"Of course I do, dear, you remind me of it at least five times every day."

"Yeah, whatever!"

As Jennifer pushed open the swing door, which allowed them access into the restaurant, both mother and daughter's jaws slackened in simultaneous surprise.

"Wow, Mum, we gotta eat!"

Jennifer looked around, truthfully she was awestruck, shocked by the cleanliness and splendor of their surroundings.

"Yes, I guess we 'gotta eat,'" she mimicked, in response to her daughter's poor grammar.

The interior of the burger bar was definitely Ying to the outside Yang. The exterior had been grubby and unkempt, with furniture and fittings decorated in a color scheme that, to Jennifer's mind, would best be described as hideous; the interior though, was something else entirely.

Jennifer had always liked modern things; there was nothing she disliked more than old kitchens in old country houses, or cottages with thatched roofs and window shutters. Actually that's not quite true, there was something she detested even more than really old things and places. If there was one thing she hated with a passion, it was new builds that were designed to appear antiquated.

Some years earlier, before Megan was born, she had won a national contest in a woman's magazine. First prize was a trip for two into London, for a show and then a meal, followed by a weekend stopover at a newly opened five star hotel called *Fifties*.

She had journeyed down with Steve on the Friday night, the two of them having been collected from their home and then transported, via chauffeur driven Bentley, straight into central London. It was a trip which had seemed heaven sent; of course this was back in the day, before she realized just what a bastard her then husband really was.

However, when they had arrived, Jennifer was horrified to discover the hotel in which they were staying had been designed as a themed venue. Polished mahogany bordered retro-colored walls, and overhead crystal chandeliers illuminated every hallway. All in an attempt to transport guests back to a bygone age.

Worse still was the discovery that the dining room was done out as some exuberantly over colorful fifties diner; complete with a jukebox in the corner which droned out repetitive sounding tunes whilst you ate. Jennifer had hated it so much, that they had left early the following evening. After booking out from Fifties they'd caught the first available train headed north out of Paddington.

However, this place in which they were now had completely taken Jennifer aback. She knew instantly that with its sharp modern design and obvious cleanliness; this was definitely her type of venue. Apart from the grey ceramic floor tiles; most of the other surfaces were brilliant white. The interior tables and chairs, at least gave the appearance of both quality and comfort, having been molded into a much sturdier design than their exterior counterparts. The atmosphere was pleasantly cool, as the slight overhead whine signaled the air conditioning was performing adequately, and although the smell of excessively grease laden food continued to loiter somewhat in the air; there was also a strong odor of disinfectant which added to the clean antiseptic atmosphere of the establishment.

Mother and daughter walked over to the food counter, where a medium built woman; kitted out in a starched, white uniform - topped off with a matching bun-hat, was standing with her back towards them, busily re-racking empty burger boxes in readiness for their presumed later requirement. As the woman heard the sound of their footsteps on the tiles she turned to greet them, a smile displayed across her round face.

Megan let out a loud titter. One which was quickly silenced by a well placed elbow to the ribs, delivered courtesy of her mother. It was fair to say though, that Jennifer herself had to bite hard into her own top lip in order to stop herself from laughing out loud.

The woman in white, who may have been in her twenties, but could just as likely have been in her thirties, was pregnant.

However, it was not in any way which Jennifer had ever seen anyone be pregnant before! To describe her 'bump' as massive just would not have done justice to her condition.

Jennifer recalled having once watched a documentary about a woman who gave birth to eight babies. Her belly had naturally been quite pronounced, but nothing like the woman's standing before them now. In all seriousness, Jennifer thought she could well have been carrying a baby elephant in her womb. She had truly never seen, or ever expected to see a sight quite like it. What made the woman look even more bizarre was how all of the bulk was being carried at the front of her body. Some women tend to naturally distribute the weight around their bodies as their pregnancy progresses, but from behind the woman in white, whose lapel badge identified her as Ellen, didn't even show as being with child.

"Hello there, may I be of service?" enquired the woman called Ellen, with her best burger bar regulation smile, whilst at the same time eyeing somewhat oddly the girl standing before her kitted out all in black. She visibly frowned at the youngster's regulation torn tights and monkey boots.

Jennifer smiled, recognizing the look on the woman's face; it was an expression she herself had often worn when her daughter first started to dress in this fashion. "You'll have to excuse my daughter's dress sense. She considers herself something of an anarchist," she quipped.

"I'm not an anarchist, I'm a Goth!"

"Well if you say so, dear."

"Actually I think it suits you, love," smiled the waitress. "So what can I get for you ladies?"

"When's your baby due?" asked Megan, ignoring the woman's request to serve them.

"Megan!" snapped her mother. "Don't be so rude!"

"It's okay, really," smiled the woman behind the counter. "To answer your question, my little one is due very soon now."

"Let's hope we get served first then, eh?" laughed Megan.

The woman behind the counter smiled politely whilst Jennifer glared at her daughter, and in such a way that it left the girl in very little doubt that she had seriously overstepped the mark.

"Please ignore my ill-mannered offspring," smiled Jennifer, apologetically. "I sometimes wonder where I went wrong."

"It's not a problem, seriously. Besides, I'm well aware that I'm carrying, somewhat… on the larger side."

The woman's pleasant manner and lack of obvious concern over Megan's flippant comments made Jennifer feel slightly better. Although she intended to give her daughter a severe reprimand later, once they were back in the privacy of the Corsa. She was used to taking all sorts of lip from the girl, but she didn't appreciate her daughter being rude to strangers; she considered that it reflected badly on her mothering skills.

Jennifer ordered two regular sized meals of French fries, cheeseburgers, two hot-apple pies, a soda for herself and banana milkshake for Megan. She had warned the girl previously about the horrendous fat content contained within such drinks, but her daughter was ever a law unto herself, and so insisted on downing the horrid stuff whenever the opportunity arose.

The woman placed two drinks onto a plastic tray, which she slid across the counter to Jennifer, before informing them that their meals would take several minutes to prepare. She told them that her husband had only just started cooking a new batch of fries, and so if they wished to take their seats she would bring their meals over to them. She then, with a surprising swiftness, reached across the counter and placed a promotional sticker of *Bertie Burger* onto the lapel of Megan's blouse. The look of indignation that appeared on the girl's face at being treated like a junior customer made Jennifer almost laugh out loud.

Thanking the woman, she promptly picked up the tray in one hand, taking a firm hold of Megan's arm with her free hand; she led her away towards a corner table - intent on removing the girl before she had time to think up any unsavory retort. If there was one thing she had learned, it was that her daughter possessed an acid tongue.

"Sit!" she ordered Megan as they reached the table, which she considered far enough removed from the counter so as any further comment made by her daughter would be safely out of earshot.

"Not yet. Need to pee!" spat Megan sarcastically, as she pointed towards a door at the back of the restaurant.

"Hurry back then, the food shouldn't be too long, and this sort of fast food only tastes any good if it's eaten while it's still warm."

"I'll piddle and be back in two minutes, okay?" quipped Megan, as she relished the look of parental despair displayed on her mother's face. Then, she turned and traipsed briskly away, before swinging open the door and exiting the eateries main area.

Alone, Jennifer sat pondering just why fate had chosen to deal out such a cruel hand; first delivering into her life such a beautiful baby daughter. However, since Steve had decided he wasn't cut out for parenting, and had left for pastures young and new, Megan had grown into such a contrary, unpleasant child.

Jennifer smiled, because one thing which gave her a degree of comfort was that Steve's new pasture was now almost eight months pregnant. He had no interest in the daughter he already had, although he begrudgingly phoned once a fortnight. He had only bothered to see Megan five times in the previous three years. Jennifer knew he'd be squirming at the prospect of being tied down as a parent once again and, since hearing the news, the old adage about *the grass always being greener* regularly crossed her mind.

Megan walked down the narrow corridor before pushing open the door and entering the ladies restroom, the door slamming shut behind her with a loud thump, its faulty closer failing to sufficiently slow its motion. She shivered slightly at the coolness of the place, even allowing for the air conditioning in the building's eatery, it still felt several degrees colder in here. Proceeding on into one of the three cubicles, she was pleased to discover that the toilets were as spic 'n' span as the rest of the joint. There had been many occasions in her young life when she had been forced, through necessity, to squat over a toilet bowl. Because, in all likelihood, any kind of physical contact with the object itself might well have resulted in contamination by some sort of ungodly germ. She still wasn't completely sure whether there was any truth to the handed down school tales of catching 'a dose' off of a toilet seat. However, it stood to reason that sitting on someone else's pee stains, or worse, was definitely unhygienic.

Megan pulled down her tights and panties and hoisted her skirt, before sitting down, and letting out a huge sigh of relief as the strong stream of urine left her body, and struck firmly against the inside of the toilet bowl, the sound resonating freely around the hollowness of the restroom. She continued to pee for what seemed to her like an eternity, although in truth it was little more than a minute. When she had finally finished emptying her bladder, Megan reached for a strip of toilet tissue and dabbed herself dry, relieved to finally be free of the discomfort, which, thanks to her mother's earlier refusal to cut short their journey, had built in the pit of her stomach.

She was in the process of rearranging her clothing, when she heard the bathroom door open for a protracted period of time, before closing once again with a loud bang. Instinctively she held her breath and listened for any movement outside of the cubicle. It was one of her foibles, but she hated using public conveniences when they were otherwise occupied. She was half expecting to hear her mother's droning voice, informing her that their food was on the table, but no one spoke. Although, the door of the compartment to her right creaked slightly as someone closed it.

Megan listened, expecting to hear movement, as her unwelcome neighbor arranged themselves onto the toilet. But all that greeted her was silence. After a minute of standing statuesque, and holding her breath to the point of turning blue in the face, Megan finally took a huge gulp of air. Balls to this, she thought, as embarrassing as it was bumping into strangers in public lavatories, it wasn't as if she had just disposed of a rancid number two! She could walk out, and hold her head high with dignity, and if the occupant of the other cubicle chose to show themselves before she had finished washing her hands, so what? Everybody has to go to the lavatory, so what was she even feeling embarrassed about?

Megan quietly unlocked the cubicle door and stepped forward towards the washbasin, turning on the mixer tap until a nice temperature of water flowed freely between her fingers. As she soaped her hands, she was conscious of the fact that still no sounds emanated from within the 'engaged' cubicle. It occurred to her that it was probably occupied by a shy, timid girl who was as uncomfortable making bodily expulsions, with others in the vicinity, as she herself was. Megan could mentally picture the young girl who was, in all probability, crouched mouse like behind the door, waiting for her to make an exit. She smiled as she pulled out a fistful of paper towels and began drying her hands. Once they were dry, Megan scrunched up the towels and threw them, with a blinding accuracy into the stainless steel waste bin positioned against the far wall.

"That's me, all done in here!" she echoed, in her loudest voice, grinning wickedly as she pictured the timorous girl behind the door, doubtless breathing a huge sigh of relief at her eminent departure.

"It's good to see that you washed your hands, sweetheart. All children should be raised to respect good standards of personal hygiene. It's very important!"

Megan let out a loud yelp of surprise at the sound of the woman's voice. Spinning around she was shocked to see Ellen, the pregnant woman from the food counter, stepping out from the alcove next to the main entrance door.

"Jesus Christ, woman!" squawked Megan. "You almost gave me a bloody heart attack!"

"Sorry, dear," replied Ellen. She smiled weakly at Megan, it was no longer the warm, friendly smile which had greeted the girl and her mother upon their arrival.

"I should go," uttered Megan, who instantly began to feel uneasy about the way in which the woman was looking her up and down with an unreadable intensity. "Listen, sorry if I said anything to offend you earlier, you know, about the baby," offered the girl, who rather uncharacteristically felt the urge to apologize.

"That's okay, Megan."

"How do you know my name?"

Ellen arched her eyebrows, quizzically, "I heard your mother refer to you earlier."

"Oh, yeah, of course you did," nodded Megan. "I should go… don't want my food to get cold, you know?"

"Don't go, Megan," implored the woman, stepping forward and blocking the girl's exit route.

Megan found herself stepping back. She still didn't quite know what it was, but her instincts told her there was something deeply unsettling about the pregnant woman before her. She was aware of the hairs standing up on the back of her neck, and an ice cold chill suddenly, inexplicably running through her veins. And yet, at the same time beads of sweat began to form across her brow.

"Do I know you?" beseeched the girl, her back now pressed firmly up against the hard ceramic washbasin. The woman's swollen belly pressing uncomfortably into the front of her.

"Megan, no, you have never known us. Indeed, you never truly could. But you, like all of your insipid, tainted kind, recalls fleeting glimpses of our majesty. Memories served of beautiful chaos contained equally within the brightest stars and your darkest nightmares! We though, know you, for we are Uvhash, rightful suitor of Shub-Niggurath, and we see all who go before us. We see all that we require within you... A selfish, embittered child, who delights in making her mother's life a living hell, and all because it helps you cope with your own suffering, your own perceived angst, with which you have managed to convince yourself that your problems alone are greater than those experienced by any other in this world... You know nothing of true pain and suffering!" The woman's words had been spoken without any noticeable emotion.

Megan wanted to yell out, to tell this fat, bloated, rambling bitch to shut her mouth and mind her own business. She wanted to tell her that she was wrong in everything she had said about her attitude and life. But Megan couldn't bring herself to respond, because she knew the words carried the sting of truth. She missed her dad, but also hated him for deserting her in favor of that skinny trollop who he was shacked up with now. Tears welled in her eyes, brought forward by thoughts of her father's failings.

"Why are you saying this stuff? What does it even mean anyway?" she blustered.

The woman chose not to acknowledge the girl's question directly, but the venom in her eyes spoke volumes.

"Oh God, please don't hurt me!" Megan heard herself saying the words, and at the very moment they had left her throat, she hated herself for sounding so weak. Okay, she decided, this whole situation was growing more surreal by the second. In fact it was getting downright bloody scary! The woman was obviously suffering some sort of mental-breakdown. However, it wasn't really likely, no matter how hard-faced the big, fat, pregnant lady was, and regardless of her seemingly having an uncanny insight into how Megan ticked... Still, it wasn't really feasible that the woman meant her any harm, was it?

"I should go," reiterated the girl, conscious that she really didn't want to spend any longer in the company of this weird woman.

"I don't think so, Megan!"

"Please, just..."

"Let you leave?" pre-empted the woman. "Don't really see that as being likely to happen, dear."

"What do you mean?"

"It is more a question of what do we need, rather than what do we mean," stated the woman, in the same emotive tone.

"Alright then," snapped Megan, her fear briefly giving way once more to her more natural character which was becoming increasingly riled by the cryptic weirdness of this odd woman who was preventing her exit. Hence, having slowly bubbled its way to the surface, Megan's temper flared. "Perhaps you should just tell me what the fucking hell it is you do want, or fucking need! And then just get the fuck out of my way, okay? Now fucking move, you stupid fat cow! And by the way, you keep referring to yourself as 'we!' What are you, fucking retarded or something?"

The woman smiled, oddly, "Ouch! Potty mouth, haven't you?"

"Get out of my way you fat bitch!" fumed Megan, while at the same time trying to force her way past her jailor. She was stunned though; the woman blocking her escape was immoveable. Try as she might Megan could not budge herself, not even an inch free of the constrictions of the woman's swollen belly.

"You asked me what I wanted. It's quite simple. I want what every other requires, and that is what is best for their self preservation!"

The woman had now seized hold of Megan's wrists, and was squeezing them in a vice tight grip.

"Please, just let me go?" begged Megan, her bravado fading as rapidly as it had arisen. Her legs felt as though they had turned to jelly, fear flooded through her, and for the first time she realized that something *really bad* was happening.

"I really wish I could, dear child. But our wants decree otherwise. We, whose display of glorious adoration Shub-Niggurath saw fit to treat with disdain. Choosing instead to abandon us as the Great Old Ones were cast back! Hence at our cost the rift was, and has remained sealed for millennia, leaving us here amongst you who are nothing, until such time as The Black Goat of the Woods with a Thousand Young returns. Though you may rest assured, the object of our appetite will return again, and our glorious union will be completed evermore! Oh, what deities we shall form from our joining. For now though, ours has need of what is yours. And later, others will have needs of what remains!"

"Oh my God, what the hell are you even talking about, you crazy—" Megan never finished her sentence. The creaking of the cubicle door distracted her, and for a moment she believed, expected, the timid little girl, whom she had imagined waiting to use the restroom in complete privacy, might spring forth to offer her some assistance in fleeing this insane woman. Or at the very least the girl would, having seen what was occurring, run screaming from the bathroom seeking out someone; anyone who was able to free her from this nightmare. But it wasn't to be…

The thing that stepped forward from behind the door was not a girl; Megan knew it could never even have been considered human! Certainly it moved in an upright fashion, although rather than arms it had a mass of writhing, thrashing tentacles which whipped ferociously about its body as it glided, slug-like across the room. It had no discernable head, although its trunk was covered with a multitude of squid-like eyes, and a beak-mouth which contained two sets of needle sharp teeth, was positioned centrally upon its torso. However, its eyes were the only feature even vaguely recognizable. Its skin, which was the color of dried blood, was not smooth, instead covered top to bottom with festering wart like abrasions, each one at least the size of a golf ball. The creature's tentacles, rather than resembling those of a squid, were more akin to thorny vines which flailed with spasmodic intensity as the aberration moved.

This fiend, whom Megan considered an escapee from hell, slithered across the ceramic tiles, moving with far more haste than its appearance would have suggested possible. When the thing had first appeared, Megan had wanted to cry out, to call for her mother's assistance. A mother who the girl now realized meant the very world to her. However, fear had stifled her voice, just for a few seconds, and by then it was too late. The monster was upon her, its razor sharp barbs ripping her flesh as tentacles moved swiftly about her body, clutching Megan in an unbreakable embrace of pain and terror. Megan panicked as she felt the intense pressure of the tendrils thrashing about her. Tears filled her eyes as her body began to come apart. She attempted to cry out as flesh and sinew were torn mercilessly from her, but her screams were muffled by the threshing appendages tearing at the flesh of her face.

It was some small degree of mercy, but the agony of the fiends attack proved to be as swift as it was brutal. Any thought the girl may have had with regards her own suffering being rapidly dispelled by the creeping sense of wonderment which overtook her. Blood and tentacles combined to obstruct oxygen from reaching vital organs, and Megan became conscious of her feet slipping away from beneath her body. A sense of floating and numbness overtook her as an array of golden lights danced merrily before her eyes, signaling the girls approaching finality. Megan realized she was no longer afraid. All sense of pain had left her, as nerve endings were stripped away and neurons failed to fire. Megan knew she would never see her mother again, and she wished that she had been a better daughter.

The pregnant woman, who had released her hold on Megan at the onset of the creatures attack, watched intently as the girl's body slid down the blood spattered washbasin, before landing with a dull thud onto the ground. The weight of the tendrils still attached to her face, increasing the harshness of the dying girl's fall.

The woman watched as the creature continued to absorb the last remaining echoes of life from Megan's limp body. She smiled, when finally having finished her work; her other released its grip on the flesh stripped corpse and stood up, turning to face Ellen.

Ellen nodded with enthusiasm. "I like it, this skin, it really suits you."

The girl held out her arms and admired the look and feel of her illusory flesh. Turning towards the bathroom mirror, she pulled various faces, taking great delight in learning how her facial muscles operated. She did this for a number of minutes, until finally she had mastered how to portray Megan Bueller's face with a smile, grimace, anger and sadness, and any other of the range of emotions it would be necessary to personify, in order for her to take on, unnoticed, the life of the poor dead girl.

"We should hurry!" noted Ellen, finally, pointing towards the corpse on the floor. "Her mother will be wondering where she is."

Nodding, the naked girl kneeled down, and began swiftly tucking the entrails back inside Megan's torn body.

"Leave that, I'll clean up in here," instructed the older woman disdainfully, as she noted the amount of bodily fluids still leaking forth from the girl's remains. "You have it in you to mimic the child's clothing?"

The girl nodded affirmation.

"Good. Proceed then." She watched silently, with tears welling in her eyes, as the further transformation occurred. It had been this way for thousands of lifetimes, and it would likely remain this way for eons more.

The Great Old Ones were gone, and for now the rift sealed.

So, mighty Uvhash, rightful suitor to Shub-Niggurath, remains trapped in this pitiful realm. But all the while The Power Internal continues to grow, and so Uvhash is forced to splinter the life essence, to tear asunder and step forward into this world in the guise of many, lest the power contained within his being should tear this planet apart!

Very soon Uvhash would be forced to expel yet more essence, and this too would be birthed as new brood. And so it was time for one more to move on, and take placement out in the wider world of mankind. Looking at the corpse on the ground, *the essence who walked as Ellen* realized it was good too, they now had some fresh flesh with which to pepper the restaurants recipes. She smiled; it pleased her greatly that those who chose to use the establishment invariably ended up congratulating them on the quality of food served. She doubted they would be quite so warm with their compliments if they knew the true origins of their meals.

Jennifer wiped her mouth with the napkin and settled back in her chair. "That was absolutely delicious," she remarked, scrunching up the tissue and placing it into the empty burger box in front of her, before emptying the last dregs of soda from her plastic cup. "What did you reckon, Megan?"

The girl smiled back across the table. "It was lovely, Mum. I really enjoyed it too. Thank you."

Jennifer smiled; giving the girl a telling off earlier had obviously done the trick. Her daughter had been on her best behavior, ever since returning from the toilets; in fact, she had been downright pleasant company, and that was most unusual. She looked around to see if she could see the pregnant waitress. She had wanted to wish her good luck with the baby, and to thank her for what was, in all probability the best burger meal she had ever eaten. But the woman had been absent since shortly after their arrival.

Jennifer sauntered over to the counter, where the rather average looking man who had earlier prepared and brought their meals over, said that his wife was busy sorting some stuff out in the back, and she would likely return shortly. After thanking him for the food, and wishing him and his spouse good fortune with the imminent birth of their child. She then enquired as to directions for getting back onto the main through route, explaining they had accidentally ended up here, due to her having gotten lost. Picking up a notepad from off the counter, the man jotted down a list of road signs and numbers that they needed to look out for, assuring them that if they followed his instructions then they would be back on a main A-road within approximately twenty five minutes. He then thanked her for her custom, and the good wishes expressed towards his unborn child. Jennifer smiled and gestured for her daughter to join her, and waving goodbye they headed out the exit. Jennifer failed to notice the look of fond farewell which passed between her daughter and the man at the counter.

Climbing into the Corsa, both mother and daughter again commented about the quality of both food and service at the restaurant, and agreed that if they ever found themselves out this way again, then they would make a return visit. Jennifer noted, with some bemusement, the level of excitement which this aroused within her daughter. As they were leaving the forecourt, Jennifer glimpsed the woman called Ellen dragging a large industrial bin liner out of the side door of the restaurant, and over towards the smaller building housing the refrigeration units. It concerned her somewhat. A woman as heavily pregnant as Ellen shouldn't be attempting to handle such heavy weights. She didn't dwell on the thought for too long though, as she knew concentration would be required, in order for her to get them back on the right road towards Glasgow.

As she pulled back out onto the country lane, Jennifer couldn't help but notice there seemed to be a different atmosphere in the car now. She glanced at the girl sitting beside her, and smiled, noting with pleasure the look of contentment upon her daughter's face. It had been a long time since she had seen the girl looking quite so happy, and it occurred to her that their day out was turning out to have been a very good idea indeed.

Kingdom Falls

A grey April afternoon cast its shadow across the courtyard below, and as far into the distance as the Princess could see a cloud of depressive melancholy rested over her city. Princess plucked a leaf from one of the plants in her mother's window box and, standing on tippy-toes, managed to drop it over the guardrail. She watched passively as it fluttered and flustered its way to the ground, some ten stories below.

She knew, because Daddy had often told her so, that they lived at the very summit of Kingdom Falls, because they were its Royal Family. Living at the top of the tower block allowed them to survey *their* entire kingdom.

Her father had told her: *'One day this will all be yours, to rule as you see fit. But always remember one thing, Princess: It is fine to have compassion in your heart, but the plebs need to be ruled with a blade of steel'.*

Princess had absolutely no idea what a *pleb* was, although she guessed it was a term applied to anyone who upsets you. She'd never known her father to use a *blade of steel*, either. But she had, on occasion, seen him use his huge fists to discipline those who lacked respect. Daddy used to take her out with him when he was collecting his *tithe* from the bars, shops, and restaurants in his kingdom. Princess liked being taken out in Daddy's car. Sitting in those plush leather seats, loud music booming out through powerful speakers and the head of every passerby turning as they drove past, it made Princess feel important.

It made her feel like a *real* princess.

Back then, most people she had ever met were kind. The shopkeepers they visited always insisted on offering sweets to Princess. The bar owners gave her soda and crisps, and even the men who came to their flat to buy Daddy's white gold, they too only ever had a kind word for the princess.

She had only ever seen Daddy get mad on a couple of occasions, and both of these were caused by bad shopkeepers refusing to pay Daddy's tithe.

Daddy had been forced to reprimand them.

Princess wiped a tear from her face.

She missed her Daddy.

She closed her eyes and tried, without success, to picture him in her mind's eye. It was odd, she could still remember everything about him, those smiling eyes, strong white teeth, diamond earring, and rings on every finger, but it was getting harder and harder now to see his face. And there weren't even any pictures of him left at home.

Not anymore.

Princess wasn't even sure how long he'd been gone now? But she did know it'd been for more than two Christmases.

Princess had actually been christened Teagan Kirsty Mckean, but even before she left the maternity room Daddy had declared her to be *his* Princess, and Daddy's word was the law.

A wet tongue slopped across the back of her calf and she looked down to see Bear's big-brown eyes fixed pleadingly on her. The pit-bull had deposited a tennis ball at her feet, and his tale was wagging excitedly as he anticipated the girl indulging his play. Princess kicked out, sending the ball racing along the walkway and the dog scooting in rapid pursuit. She giggled as she watched her best and *only* friend clatter into the two sun chairs positioned outside no. 1009, sending them rattling down the landing as he retrieved the ball. The dog returned with his trophy, and at the command of a raised forefinger he dropped the ball to the floor and awaited a fresh chase.

As she sent the animal on a repeat quest Princess recalled the day Daddy first brought the dog home. A bundle of brindle fun for his girl to love, and who, in turn, would always serve and protect his little mistress.

Shouting coming from inside the flat reminded her just how much things had changed during the last few years. When Daddy had first gone away both she and Mummy had been sad. They had both cried lots. Life had been tough. And people who had always been kind in the past were unfriendly now. She didn't know when Daddy would come home, but she'd heard two women in the street saying they *doubted Paul McKean would be back in their lifetime.*

Princess was just relieved the women were old.

Their lifetimes would be fairly short.

Snide and uncalled for comments were bad enough, but other people were downright scary!

Some of the *white snow* men kicked in the door to their flat. They locked Bear in the kitchen, and then they took Mummy into the bedroom and upset her.

Mummy cried for two days after they left.

The child had tried her best to console her mother, but the woman just kept saying these were bad men, and that they stank.

Princess guessed this to be the reason Mummy took so many showers during those bad days.

She was still a month short of her seventh birthday, but even so Princess could recognize those to have been dark times. As the dog once again deposited the ball and a sizeable quantity of drool at her feet, Princess noted the shouts from inside becoming louder, and she wondered if these days were really any brighter?

When Christian had first appeared on the scene, Mummy seemed happy for the first time since Daddy went away. He used to bring sweets with him for Princess and treats for Bear, and Mummy smiled and laughed a lot. It only took a few months before Christian moved into the flat, and within a few weeks things had began to change. He took to kicking Bear and shouting at Princess. And on at least three occasions Princess had seen him punching her mother. There were other times too, when Mummy displayed unexplained scratches and bruises. He'd once raised a hand to Princess, but Bear had placed himself between man and girl, and there'd been enough of a warning displayed in the dog's eyes for the man to desist.

Princess hated Christian.

She wanted him gone from their lives.

Unfortunately, that would never happen now.

In February, her mother had given birth to twins. Princess had been fascinated with the boys, surprised at just how small and inactive they were over the early weeks of their lives.

Two months on and they were starting to show more awareness, although it was proving difficult for Princess to fully bond with them as they so resembled their father. They also took up an awful lot of Mummy's time.

But they did retain certain cuteness.

The sound of the front door opening caused her to turn around, only to find herself confronted by a towering male figure. Perspiration stained the underarms of Christian's yellow t-shirt, and a familiar white powder caked his unshaven top lip.

"You throwing stones over that balcony again?" he glared.

Princess shook her head.

"Get inside now. And bring that mutt with you."

■■

She sat ramrod still on a pink breakfast stool, her interlocked fingers resting on the Formica surface of the kitchen worktop. Bear rested by her feet. Princess stared through the open door into the lounge, eyeing the adults impassively as they bottle fed the boys. Not a word exchanged between them, and yet fear was palpable in the air.

Princess had come in off the landing complaining she was hungry, and had asked Mummy if they could eat lunch soon. Mummy and Christian had already been arguing, and the girl's request had acted as a catalyst for a further outburst. Christian insisted *his little men of the house* should be fed before the girl. Mummy had pointed out they weren't due another feed for an hour yet. This comment had earned her a split lip. She might well have received further chastisement had Bear not chosen to emit an uncharacteristic growl.

It was enough to stem the violence.

Eventually Christian spoke. "If that dog keeps acting out he'll have to go.

"No!" Princess almost sobbed, running into the lounge and throwing her arms about her mother's shoulders. "He can't, Daddy gave Bear to me."

"Hush, child," reassured her mother. "I'm sure Bear will be fine."

"I'm telling you," said Christian, the cruel half-smile that had crept onto his face evaporated into a look of distain as his gaze fixed towards the animal, "either it learns some respect for me, or it's out of here!"

"Mummy?"

"Hush girl, now is not the time. Just take Bear to your room and leave us to sort the babies."

The curtains were pulled back and Princess chose to lay in silence, wallowing in the dullness of a slate sky, her arms straddling the dog curled beside her. Over the course of the following hours she heard her mother and Christian laughing. It always seemed to be the same. Violent rows followed by bouts of exaggerated bliss. She heard Mummy declaring *stinky winky!* as she cleaned up the messy diapers of her *little angels*. Christian repeatedly made silly cooing noises at his *precious little men,* and the twins throats emitted gurgles of self-centered satisfaction at the attention lavished upon them.

∎∎

She was woken by the sound of the front door closing. The clock beside her bed declared the time to be 6:15pm. Someone had been into her room and drawn the curtains, and Bear no longer slept beside her.

Her tummy rumbled with pangs of hunger, and Princess slid herself down off the bed, wiping sleepy dust from the corners of her eyes as she did so.

She pulled on a pair of pumps and walked through into the lounge, where she found her mother asleep on the sofa. A dull cloud of blue/grey smoke still loitered close to the ceiling and a number of Mummy's *special smokes* were burnt out in the ashtray. A search of the apartment revealed the twins to be asleep in the bedroom which they shared with their parents, snoozing gently in their cot. Bear was nowhere to be found, and worryingly neither was Christian.

Princess experienced a sudden and unexplained feeling of unease sweeping through her, and for reasons she couldn't fully fathom, she bolted out the front door and onto the landing.

Grabbing the guardrail she hoisted herself up on tip-toes and looked to the courtyard below. Christian was two thirds of the way across the diagonal, heading towards the exit which led onto the parkland. Bear was trotting along beside him on a loose leash.

Christian had never before taken Bear for a walk, because Christian never liked Bear.

■■■

By the time Princess had ridden the elevator to the ground floor both man and dog were out of sight, but instinct, or maybe logic, drove her pursuit in the right direction. The route Christian had taken offered only two options, left up towards the high road or right onto open fields.

Princess opted for the parklands.

The evening had actually turned into the nicest part of the day. Clouds had broken, and then faded leaving a pale, clear sky. The sun hadn't even been a contender, and now sank towards the horizon, a defeated blister succumbing to the full moon rising.

Princess spotted Christian and the dog in the distance on the high ground, a series of hills and hollows which fed away from the main parkland. Princess called out, but neither man nor dog appeared to hear her.

She was too far away.

The girl broke into a run, tripping and stumbling her way over the uneven ground. Twice she fell down. But on both occasions she climbed to her feet and continued to run.

Princess wasn't sure why, but she knew that she needed to reach Bear.

Finally clearing the hills and hollows, she stopped in her tracks. At the far side of the next field Christian had taken a right, and was leading the dog up and over the railway bridge.

Where is he taking Bear?

This made no sense at all to Princess. The housing estate on the far side of the tracks was, according to grownups she had overheard, one of the roughest parts of the city. Even Daddy took *friends* with him whenever he had business to do there. Princess was breathing heavily and her pace had slowed almost to a walk, but she kept her eyes fixed towards the man and dog as they surmounted the overpass. Her approach brought her parallel to the tracks, and she was surprised that Christian, who had stopped midway across the bridge and was now leaning against the handrail, failed to notice her closing on his position.

He seemed lost in a far place.

Bear though, stooped his shoulders, and peered through the acrylic barrier edging the walkway. Even at a distance Princess could see his tail wagging, and hear the excitable serenade which he emitted whenever they shared a reunion.

Princess smiled, *Bear has spotted me.*

It happened so fast that Princess had time neither to react nor scream. Christian closed the distance between himself and the dog, grabbed Bear by the collar and, with one hand under the animal's belly, scooped him up from the ground, and threw him over the railing.

The dog yelped as it plummeted from the bridge, and there followed a dull thud, then silence.

For what seemed an age, Princess stood rooted to the spot, tears welled in her eyes, her body was cold and she shook uncontrollably, but her legs wouldn't allow her to run to the railings. She wanted to go to bear, but her body refused to let her move in the direction of the shattered creature laying on the tracks.

And then she heard the dog whimper, and suddenly she found the will to move. Princess raced along the railings looking for any point of access. She found one strut which had been dislodged at its base, no doubt to allow local kids entrance onto the tracks. Princess was a slim girl and passed easily through the gap, thorny bushes edging the line ripped swathes from her flesh, but she didn't stop.

There was movement out towards the middle of the tracks, she'd found him. Bear was lying on his side, but his head was raised and he cried out in pain. Princess moved forward wanting to go to him, but as she stepped across the first set of rails she stopped. She remembered what Daddy had once told her. *Some of the tracks on a rail line can kill you.*

What should I do?

It was a question destined to remain unanswered.

She'd barely noticed the rumble before the locomotive appeared, thundering its way towards the bridge and the stricken dog. The velocity and proximity of the passing train almost forced her off her feet. Her hair whipped and she instinctively closed her eyes, clenching her fists as the passing disturbance of dust and grit pummeled about her.

When she opened her eyes Bear was gone.

She stood ramrod stiff. A stream of urine ran down her legs, warm against the shock impacting her body.

Princess stood in silence for a long time, her watery eyes desperately searching the tracks for the marvel of Bear's return.

It was a miracle fated never to happen.

She tried to understand how anyone could ever do something so evil? Bear had never done anything bad in his life. All he ever desired was to receive affection, and he offered nothing but unconditional love in return. Princess hated Christian more than she ever had.

Christian was a *pleb*. And one day he would pay for what he'd done.

As Princess entered the front door, which had been left ajar, she could hear the policeman asking questions of Christian and her mother. The officer was perched on the edge of an armchair. Christian shared the sofa with Mummy, a consoling arm wrapped around her shoulders. Another officer was standing taking notes, and occasionally talking into his radio.

The hallway was in darkness and none of the adults noticed as Princess listened in silence. Mummy had awakened to find her daughter gone, and after a search of the surrounding areas which had failed to recover the girl, she'd been forced to call in the police to find her missing child. Mummy told lies, claiming Christian had never left home, and that he only woke up after Mummy raised the alarm.

No one noticed Princess slipping back into the shadows. She edged her way along the hall, into Mummy's bedroom. The twins were sleeping, the burped smell of milk confirming they'd recently been fed. Princess leaned into the cot, marveling at the fluttering eyelids of her baby brothers, tiny faces twitching as they dreamed of warm milk and clean diapers.

Placing an arm carefully under one brother, she cradled his head with her free hand and scooped him up into her arms, standing transfixed by the tiny features of the infant she now held. It was with some difficulty but she managed to lift the second child too.

Although at one point she almost dropped both infants. The relief was palpable when finally she held them securely. One of the boys opened his eyes and smiled at Princess, and it occurred to her that this was actually the first time the baby had seemed to recognize her. This gave a warm feeling inside, and she felt her heart flutter with appreciation for her little brother.

Moving to the bedroom door, she listened to make sure the adults were still occupied in the lounge. Then, once she was certain of remaining undiscovered, she moved through the shadows towards the still open front door, gently soothing the boys as she carried them.

Outside on the landing, the temperature had cooled and a chill wind ruffled the trio. Princess wished she'd taken the time to put on a thicker top. From the courtyard below teen banter disturbed the peace of the evening, and the joyful shouts made Princess wish for a life she'd never known. The twins were already beginning to weigh heavy, and Princess moved to the guardrail, using it as an assist to support the boys. Her brother had woken again, and was once more smiling up at her. She leaned forward and kissed his forehead. And for the first time she realized Christian was right.

These *were* precious little men.

She took a sharp breath of cold air, and with one forced effort heaved the child high onto her shoulder before throwing him over the railing. From somewhere at ground level, a female voice screamed as the child plummeted. And as a crumpling thud, and the triggering of a car alarm, suggested impact with a vehicle below, all hell broke loose. Horrified cries echoed around the courtyard, and from inside the flat Princess was conscious of the hall light being turned on. The child in her arms was still sleeping. She was thankful for this mercy. In one movement she kissed him and released him over the balcony, standing on her tippy-toes to watch his descent towards the howling throng in attendance.

By the time the first the policeman had reached Princess and dragged her clear of the rail, her mother was lying on the landing screaming, eyes far away, lost in a distant mist. Christian was looking over the ledge towards the horror beneath, knuckles white as he gripped the bar for support.

"What have you done? What have you done? My God, what have you done?" the second officer's cries failed to make any impression on Princess.

Christian turned and looked to her, his face twisted by grief, a whisper on his lips, "Why?"

The girl's mouth curved, a smile which failed to hide the contempt she felt for the man before her. She did not answer his question.

Every Single Night (Original Flash Fiction Narrative)

The following flash fiction narrative was written as homage to James Herbert: 1943-2013.

It's always the same… every single night… since we moved into the countryside.

We hear the commotion…

My wife opens the patio doors…

Rushes out into the garden… and chases Moxie around, before finally pinning him on the ground…

In a futile attempt to save the mouse trapped in his jaws.
Sometimes, he has a little bird.

Once, he even caught a bat.

Afterwards - when the mouse has met its end - my wife won't talk to Moxie.

Other than to tell him he's a nasty piece of work... and then she moans at me... lots! She says I should have done more to help.

To be honest, she hasn't stopped moaning since we were forced out of London. You see, she wanted to stay behind...

I wish she had!

Unfortunately, the authorities insisted that we leave... everybody had to leave.

It was safer that way.

Last night, commotion... She opened the doors, and ran into the garden...

Sometime later... I looked out.

Moxie was up a tree, and my wife? Well, she was on the ground wrestling with four rats...

Really - really big rats! Like the rats we saw as we left London.

I closed the patio doors... her screams were becoming quite disturbing.

Then I cracked open a beer and turned on the television...

Match of the Day would be starting shortly.

But before it started, I just had time to search through the cupboards for my wife's life insurance policy.

Sweet Sugar

My legs are beginning to ache, but I maintain a steady gait which carries me briskly along the winding country lane. I turn up the collar on my coat, every exhaled breath billows in the night air, and I wish I'd remembered to wear my gloves. I wish too that I'd worn thicker socks.

The road is bordered on one side by a forest of formidable looking oaks, and even though I have traversed this route many times over the years, still the night serves to present these ancients with a discernable quality of unpleasantness, suggesting their latent ability to present threats unknown. It is, of course, just presumed threats, and a feeling of ill which quickly evaporates with dawn's first light. Still though, I cast them a glance, and an icy shudder runs through me. To my right, beyond the hedgerows, the landscape slopes away into an expanse of rural splendor, and further still in the distance, a stretch of sluggish black water purls in the moonlight.

The slightest hum draws my attention skywards, an airliner, its lights winking across an ocean of frozen stars, no doubt delivering its cargo of expectant passengers to some exotic locale. No doubt too, some of those aboard will find that exotic isn't always as described in the brochure.

I check my watch, and I'm surprised to find that it is past midnight. I tap the dial, the second hand is still moving, and I am annoyed that it has taken me this long. Sugar will be worried. I quicken my stride…

I begin to feel better once the eerie copse is behind me. Foolish I know, but when it's dark the place gives me the creeps. Not that I'd ever let Sugar know that I was scared of the trees.

Sarah Reeson. That was her name back then, but to me she will always be Sweet Sugar. She's always been a free spirit. She's always been strong willed too. If I'm to be absolutely honest about it, she can be bloody hard work at times. But she is who she is, and I love her to bits. I always will.

The very first time I laid eyes on Sugar, well I was barely into my first term at Uni, summer had arrived late that year, and when it finally did arrive it provided one of those rarities of nature which we British fondly refer to as a scorcher. Of course, as is usually the case with our nation, after just a few weeks of sunshine people began moaning about the extreme heat. Doubtless, within a couple of months those same people would be the ones moaning about the cold, but such is life.

Anyway, due to the heat, many of the students liked to use their break periods as an opportunity for improvised tanning sessions. There was a grassy oval at the front of the study centre, and the fact the oval was bordered by bounteous sycamores, allowed for a degree of shade for those who preferred some protection from the sun's onslaught. Sugar, well she was a sun worshipper. The temperature had climbed into the mid – eighties by first recess, and many of the students opted to stay inside, enjoying the comfort of the air conditioned buildings. Those who did venture out sought shade beneath the trees, but not Sugar.

She was sitting on a blanket, and she knew she looked a vision. All the boys had eyes only for her, even the lads with girlfriends in tow; they couldn't help but cast furtive glances in Sugar's direction, and always with looks which showed their own desperation to hide their wanton deception from the chosen by their side.

She wore white shorts, which could just as easily have qualified as panties, and a matching sports bra. Her luxuriant, dark hair stretching halfway down her back and complementing perfectly her sun – bronzed skin. She was lithe, everything toned and finely lined. I watched as she groomed herself, admiring every elegant movement carried out for her adoring public.

From the embossed silver case beside her she withdrew scissors, polishes, emery boards and files. Carefully, and with a delicate finesse, she set about her work with the precision of a manicurist. I watched her, mesmerized, and time evaded me. I knew I was going to be late for my next lesson because the lawn had all but cleared, but I didn't care, I had to stay.

She had begun painting her toenails by the time I plucked up the courage to approach her. Back then, and amongst my peers, I was renowned for my confidence, some might say cockiness. If they could have seen me then, I was a wreck!

I closed the distance approaching her from behind, "Hi there," my opening line.

With slow deliberate strokes of the brush she painted another toenail red, completely ignoring my opening gambit.

Then I said it, the stupidest chat up line I'd ever uttered, and to this day I still have no idea why I said it. Yes, I'd heard it in some movie, but it sounded cool then. "You're a real good looking girl, do you know that? Sitting there, you look just as sweet as sugar."

The laughter which returned in my direction broke me; I recognized no mirth, only ridicule.

"That was a real crap effort!" she scolded.

At that point I did what any self respecting seventeen year old would do given those circumstances, and beat a hasty retreat with laughter still stinging my ears. A harsh beginning and I was just glad no one else had witnessed her rebuke. By the time lessons were over I had chalked it off to experience and convinced myself she was way out of my league anyway. So, just imagine my surprise when I left Uni that evening and found Sugar waiting for me by the main gates!

I was horrified at first; I had four mates with me and was petrified the girl was going to hand me another verbal thrashing in front of my pals.

Instead, she walked over and placed a folded note into my hand, then whispered into my ear, "You're quite cute, but seriously need better chat up lines! You've got my number so give me a call, and try to do better next time."

With that she turned on her heels and disappeared into the throng of departing students. To this day I still don't know who was more dumbstruck, but regardless of whether it was my friends or me, that was the beginning of something very special. Obviously from day one she insisted I call her Sugar, and regularly delighted in embarrassing me by telling anyone who would listen of my famous chatting up techniques, but I didn't care. God I love that woman!

I check my watch as I reach the perfection of our white picket fence. I never considered myself overly skilled at working wood, but the border of our property stands as an exercise in geometric wizardry; at least it does in my eyes. The time is seventeen minutes past midnight. Damn the late shift!

As I step onto the driveway my face is calm, but inside me a rage begins to burn, and I don't know why?

I walk past the lawn which is laid as impressively as any bowling green.

The bungalow itself is an esthetic building, all white with a carved cornice enhancing the eaves and similarly styled window surrounds adding to the metrical features of the place. The drive runs alongside the property, but I only proceed down half its length before stopping at the front door, where two pudgy-faced gnomes stand on guard. Sugar loves gnomes.

The front of the property is in darkness, and as I fight to pull my keys free from my coat pocket I hear a sound. I stop and listen. Again, a cry, but it is a short broken sound and I am not certain of its point of origin?

Moving back from the front door I step once more onto the drive, straining my ears into the night. At first I hear nothing. Then I do…

The cry rises and I feel sick in the pit of my stomach. The woman's voice is not registering any pain. It is not that sort of cry.

I move further up the drive, towards the rear of the property. The blinds are drawn but the light from a bedside lamp presents a silhouette of all which I need not see. She is positioned astride him, and I am forced to close my eyes. Tears begin burning my cheeks as my ears bear witness to their crime. At one point she calls out his name but it is lost to me. Sugar has always been a free spirit, but never in this way. Was our love ever as special as I'd believed?

Eventually all falls silent and the bedside lamp is extinguished. I strain my ears, listening for any conversation which may grant me a clue as to who this infiltrator might be. But all is quiet. And all is still.

I slide my hands into the pockets of my coat and I realize I can no longer feel my fingers. My eyes stare at the now darkened window, my face is expressionless, the only clue to my inner turmoil provided by the dried tracks of my tears. I should enter now. I should take a knife from the kitchen draw and mete out a suitable brand of justice. But I would never do that to Sugar. I could never do that to Sugar. If she chooses him over me what can I do, other than love her and set her free? I'll go inside and confront them. I'll tell them that I know it all, and I'll tell Sugar she needs to make a choice. But what if she chooses him? I'll go inside… soon.

The glare from the car's headlights blinds me momentarily, and I am forced to shield my eyes as the vehicle maneuvers up the tight driveway and moves slowly towards me. Inside the bungalow the main bedroom light flicks on and I think I spy a face at the window. Have Sugar and her lover realized I've rumbled them, and have they called in some heavies who he knows, thugs who will dish out a beating to me?

The vehicle dips to side lights and the passenger door opens. I feel confused and tense and I wonder what unpleasantness is about to follow?

"Dad? Are you okay, dad?"

It's a sweet voice, and as she moves towards me I see she has a sweet face too. The driver exits the car but hangs back. At this stage, and for no particular reason, it occurs to me that the stonework of the bungalow now looks dirty.

She takes my hands in hers. "Dad, we've been worried to death about you!"

I don't know her, but she has warm hands and a comforting touch. She squeezes my hands gently and it feels safe.

"Sugar's in there!" I gesture towards my home.

"No, she's not dad, Mum's at home. Sugar's at home."

"I don't understand?"

She squeezes tighter, "I know you don't. It's okay. You've just been getting a bit confused, that's all. This was your home twenty five years ago, dad. You and mum moved from here years back. The whole family has been out looking for you."

"I don't want Sugar to leave me!"

"She never will, dad. None of us will ever leave you."

I notice that she's beginning to cry, and I recognize that she has her mother's eyes. Somewhere, within the recesses of my mind a name springs up, and I chance that it is her name, "Sally?"

"Dad," she throws her arms round my neck and hugs me and it feels good. "I love you, dad."

"Sally, can we go home now?"

"Yes, dad, we can. It's time we got you back to Sugar."

They help me into the back of the car, and she climbs in beside me and holds my hands in hers. It feels good. It feels safe.

As he reverses off the drive, I appreciate the warmth of the vehicles interior, and I remember that his name is Paul. He works as a car mechanic and he is a good man. He is married to my daughter.

I have a feeling of deja-vu and it sickens me. My head is pounding, and through the sifting cloud of my memories I come to see that this is not the first time events such as these have played out in my life. It has happened before.

I am scared.

I know the darkness is closing in, and one day soon I will be lost to it forever. For now though, I just want to go home. I need to cherish whatever time is left, and to be held, safe in the arms of my Sweet Sugar.

Aphrodite Tears

You can never escape your nature. I remember my father saying those words to me. But my father was always a good man.

Was I truly a bad man? Or had I just succumbed to nature?

The alley was in darkness.

I had always preferred the shadows. The rain had lightened, but still puddles settled on the ground. As she approached I knew this was my time to talk with her. I had been watching for days. Waiting for the right moment to tell her how she makes me feel. I shall tell her of how we should be together, partners in life, partners in love…

She just laughs at me!

Haven't they always laughed at me?

I don't even remember having placed the stiletto into my coat pocket.

Maybe something demonic placed it there?

Or maybe my carrying of it is nature?

My fist closed around the handle. She was still laughing as the shank pierced her gut. She clutched her stomach and stumbled backwards, and for the first time I realized her full radiance. She looked at me through those big beautiful eyes. The look she wears is almost one of apology as she crumples to the floor. I look down and smile. I see her now, and she is a picture. She lies on her back; a Naiad reclined on a bed of pooled water.

Hair falls loose about her head, a halo framing Aphrodite's beauty.

Her coat has fallen open revealing a white silk blouse, centred by an ever increasing crimson Rorschach. The skirt is cut above the knee, and has ridden up past her thighs to reveal a glimpse of marble white flesh. Her stockings are black. Her breasts are ample. Her lips are scarlet. She is beautiful. I part her knees and kneel between them, unzipping myself as I do so. Her breathing is shallow but steady. I lean forward and kiss her rose lips, and it is the sweetest thing I have ever known. And as I push my love into her she lets out a slight moan and tries to speak. I can't make out her words. It doesn't matter because I love her.

I have always loved her.

I always love them!

As I push deeper the breathing changes, her gasps becoming ragged. I close my hands around her neck, and squeeze.

I race to finish before she succumbs.

She surprises me.

Her hands run up my back, from buttocks to shoulders, and then fingers begin pulling at my hair. She can no longer breathe. But rather than struggle she chooses to pull me closer, her tongue pressing into my mouth. She kisses me hard, and I lighten my grip on her throat.

My pace quickens. Harder. Deeper. Faster.

Water splashes in the puddles beneath us, and I feel a tightening at the wetness of our conjoined core. My head grows dizzy, and the world ceases to exist beyond our rhythm.

I pant for breath…

She is amazing.

I thrust deeper and deeper, and every nerve is alive as her groans urge me on. Every thrust is accompanied by the sensation of being absorbed into a vacuum, and it feels incredible until… finally…

Completion.

As I orgasm I am aware of her blissful cries. She too celebrates the fulfilment of our union. We lie together, panting. I feel odd. I don't know why. But I know that I love her, and I whisper this fact.

Once again, she emits a disdainful laugh. She places her hands to my chest and easily forces me away. I fall backwards landing with a bump on the ground. My head is dizzy and I feel sick.

I am surprised to see my love so readily rise up. The wound to her stomach no longer seems to trouble her, but an abundance of blood stains her vulva and thighs. I look down past my hips, to see if I too have blood on me.

And I scream the cry of a man who has been forced to submit everything.

She brushes at the deep stain on her blouse. Tut-tutting as she chastises me for ruining a favourite garment. I remain seated on the ground, transfixed by the blood pooling between my legs.

Having straightened her upper clothing she turns and approaches me, and with skirt hoisted, positions that dark triangle inches from my face. She parts the lips of her vulva, and using a finger and thumb withdraws the trophy she has torn from me.

She drops the penis into my lap, and my cry is less than a whimper.

She chooses to stroke the back of her fingers across my face. The action suggests contrition. The tone, and her words, suggests otherwise, "I should forgive you, darling. None of us are capable of escaping who we are. But your nature presents as an affront to womankind." She leans in and kisses me, once on the mouth. "Goodbye, my love."

Aphrodite walks away, leaving me to bleed out alone. But I forgive her… because I love her.

Losing Him

If I'm honest with myself, I should never have married him. The age thing was always going to be a problem; at least I realized that fact now. This though, wasn't the major issue. What was more of a problem was the fact that he was a womanizing prick. Of course, it's my own fault because almost everyone I knew warned me what he was like.

As I turn off the gas, and lift the saucepan away from the hob, I marvel at how even now, I can remember those times as if they were only yesterday. The first day I started working there I hated it, but jobs were scarce, and Uncle Jack had a vacancy in the butcher's shop which he owned. He said they would train me up to become a skilled tradesperson. I can still remember those first few weeks, the smell of the meat made me want to vomit. I wouldn't have even stayed, if it hadn't of been for him. I was a fool really, just a young girl blinded by the rapier wit, and social acumen of this older guy. Back then, he seemed so very gentle and kind. Little did I realize, of course, that this was just his manner whenever he was anywhere near the ladies. At least until he had wormed his way into their affections, at which point the violent, sadistic bully usually decided to put in a show stopping appearance.

I look towards the dining table. He sits there silently, waiting for me to serve his dinner. The silence is almost deafening, and I know that I'm losing him. I wish he understood. I want to tell him how much I care. Except every time I attempt such a conversation, it ends in a fit of screaming rage. He seems to delight in telling me that it's entirely my fault. My stomach knots and I tell myself that it's just his angst, and that he doesn't really blame me. Does he?

I scoop the green beans out of the pan, dividing them into two equal portions onto the plates set on the worktop. Without meaning to, I let out a deep sigh. "Why?" I ask myself, barely audible.

"Because it's your fault!" those words again, but at least this time they are said in a whisper.

I don't respond, choosing instead just to hold my tongue. I don't want another shouting match. Not now, not with him!

I turn out the oven, and remove the tray containing the joint of meat and the roast potatoes. As I turn to set the tray down on the work surface, I catch a fleeting glimpse out of the corner of my eye. The way he is staring at me, like he is attempting to unravel the layers of my soul. A shudder runs right through me, as just for a minute I allow myself to wonder if he knows. But no, I am just being paranoid.

"You shouldn't have done it!"

I close my eyes and say a silent prayer. 'Please God; don't let him start again, not now.'

Turning to face him, our eyes lock, and I find myself unable to speak the words of affirmation that I so desperately want to say to him. We stare at each other for what seems an age, in truth it is barely a minute. Finally, our impasse is broken; a loud knocking on the back door succeeds in re-focusing my attention on the world.

The door swings open, and without waiting for the courtesy of an invitation into my parlor, the fat police sergeant, with the handlebar moustache, meanders into the centre of the room; without even having the decency to first wipe his boots upon the doormat. I stare angrily at the muddy prints that have stained my hardwood floor. The policeman is either oblivious or ignorant of his crime, and so I choose to once again hold my tongue.

"Just to let you know, luv. We've completed our search of the garden, and we're packing up now."

'Luv,' who was he calling 'luv?' "And?" I ask, somewhat aggressively.

"And we didn't find anything, luv."

"Of course you didn't!" Of course they didn't. I was the one who reported my philandering husband missing. Did they really believe I was likely to have murdered him, and then disposed of his body in our own back garden? It's no wonder this country is going down the pan, if that's the best that the police can come up with. He's been gone almost ten weeks now, and suddenly they decide to 'Titchmarsh' my garden.

"Do you mind if we carry on?" I ask, gesturing towards the half served up dinners on the work surface.

"No, luv, you carry on. It smells lovely." He lumbers across the room, scattering more droplets of soil as he goes. I manage to force a smile, only allowing myself to grimace once he has cleared the room.

My son sits silently at the table, a look of glaring distain aimed permanently at me. As I carve the joint onto the plates, I can almost feel his eyes burning into the back of my neck, and I wished that I could tell him what a pig his father had been, but that would never be fair.

We'd been married for slightly less than two years the first time I caught him out. The last time was not so very long ago. He had gone over the road, to help Mrs. Turner move some furniture around. I had my doubts. The woman had always had a dodgy reputation. He'd been gone for almost an hour, when I decided to go and investigate. They should have at least had the sense to drop the latch; I found them in the lounge. There he was, trousers around his ankles, and Mrs. Turner on her knees attempting to deal with his fatty. I just turned and walked away, and he just watched me leave. It was almost two hours later before he came home, obviously he decided to stay and finish the job!

I too was on my knees by the time he returned home, decided to do a bit of potting in the garden. I thought that it might have helped to clear my head, but it hadn't. He told me that I was the love of his life, his everything, and that what he had done didn't mean a thing. It did to me though, and I'd heard it all so many times before. We argued, and I called him a man whore, but that's not true though. He'd been *giving it away* for years. I'm not quite sure at what point I first struck him. I'm not sure now whether I was even aware that I still had the trowel in my hand. I hit him in the stomach, and he sank to his knees. At first he swore at me, and then as the blood began to seep through his shirt, he begged for my assistance. I remembered my training, and my second blow landed hard against his throat. I watched dispassionately as he quickly bled out.

It was strange how calm I'd managed to stay that day, I marvel at that fact even now. He wasn't a big man, but nevertheless he took some moving.

"You okay, mum?"

I smile. It was the first time in weeks that my boy had spoken to me in such an angelic tone. Maybe I wasn't losing him. "Yeah, I'm fine," I whisper, nodding at him in affirmation as I do so.

As I set our meals on the table, and sit down alongside my son, it occurs to me that life can be strange in the way it works things out. Sure, I'd married a pig, but out of that union I had been blessed with a beautiful child.

Out of the window I can just see the policemen clearing away the canvas tarpaulins, which they've had spread around my garden. I hadn't worried; the large torrents of rain that had been afflicting the country meant that any evidence that had possibly been there, would by now, have been washed away.

As we tuck into our meal, I say another silent prayer, this time blessing Uncle Jack for having died a childless bachelor. I thank him too for having left his shop to me. Not that I harbored any desire to work in a butchers shop. In fact since Jack's death, two years earlier, and due to the current economic climate, the shop had been standing desolate and empty. It had turned out to be a blessing for me that the buildings refrigeration units were still working, within the cold store. Of course, it was also a blessing that virtually no one was even aware of my owning the place.

I watch as my son tucks in heartily, wolfing down large mouthfuls of roast potato and beans, and then I smile as he starts on his meat. The enjoyment on his face is plain to see, even though he has been angry at me for driving his father away. Still though, he has continued to enjoy his meals, being especially fond of that which has become the staple of our diet. The meat is like sweet pork, with an added flavor of poultry. Definitely it's an acquired taste, but nonetheless a pleasant one. He blames me for his father going, and maybe he always will, but as I watch him clear his plate I so desperately want him to know, that even though his father has gone, he has not gone far. I have always believed it to be right, that a child should have both parents with them. After all, that is what family is all about.

Preview:

Carmilla
The Wolves of Styria

Joseph Sheridan Le Fanu

And

David Brian

A letter written by Doctor Alvinci, addressed to Baron Vordenburg. Dated *August 10th, 1860*

Dear Baron Vordenburg,

I write in the hope that you will remember meeting my good self; we were introduced at a garden party at the home of the Baroness von Waxensteini, almost three years ago.

It may help your memory of me if I tell you that I am a rather tall individual, standing several inches higher than the average Austrian male; a fact which you yourself commented on. The two of us spent some hours in conversation, in part because it became apparent that we shared a number of similar interests, particularly in all subjects esoteric. Things, that if I might say, you are substantially more adept at than myself. Although I should also mention that since last we spoke I have had experience of what I believe to have been a revenant, and unfortunately that incident did not end at all well for the young lady involved. I can assure you that the situation, with which I am now confronted, far outweighs that which has gone before. It is for this very reason that I write you now, as I feel sure that your expertise is needed in order to cleanse this district of a most despicable evil.

I am myself new to this area, having only arrived a fortnight earlier, and that at the behest of my good friend and colleague Doctor Spielberg. He knew of my interest in the arcane and he hoped, vainly as it transpired, that I may have been able to resolve the growing unpleasantness which surrounds us.

I will tell you now some of the strange and repugnant happenings which have been afflicting these lands, in the hope that you may be able to offer some guidance as to how these matters should be proceeded with.

For several weeks now this district has been subjected to a most mysterious malady, one which for the most part, but not always, tends to afflict females and usually then being girls within a certain range of ages. I myself had only been here for a number of days, when Doctor Spielberg suggested that I accompany him on his rounds as he was due that morning to visit

Analiese Dorner, she being the young wife of a local swineherd, Bruno.

Analiese had some days earlier, claimed to have woken from her sleep to find something heavy attached to her throat. She fought desperately to free herself, as she felt, in her words, "that the very life was being throttled out of her." Then, without any obvious reason, the fiend released her. Sitting upright, she saw a darkly dressed figure on the far side of the room, near the door. For one brief moment she thought that she saw a female face staring back at her from under the cowl, and just as quickly the apparition was gone. Analiese spent some minutes trying to wake her husband, a light sleeper, from his position on the bed beside her, but was unable to rouse him. And within just a short time, she felt a strange melancholy sweeping through her body, debilitating her strength, and she quickly lapsed into a deep, but fitful sleep.

Doctor Spielberg and I arrived at the Dorner's modest dwelling, at just past midday; a worried looking Bruno greeted us upon our arrival. After a brief conversation, in which he largely despaired at his wife's continuing decline, we followed him inside to where his bedridden wife lay.

I must confess to having been shocked. Analiese, although bereft of any powders, as would be expected for a woman of her standing, nonetheless, she was a creature of beauty. Or at least it was plain to see that she once had been. A thick mop of brown hair, streaked with layers of blonde, adorned her crown and hung down over her shoulders. Her skin though had a pallid complexion, and though she smiled to acknowledge our arrival, her eyes remained dull and lifeless. I took hold of her wrist, to check her pulse, and found the touch clammy beyond reason. Analiese's heart beat steadily, although her breathing remained shallow. She had no fever. Neither did she suffer from any pockmarks, or other rashes elsewhere on her body. The only mark we did find was the tiniest blue bruise on her neck, at precisely the point where she described the strangulation as having commenced.

We questioned the woman at length, where upon Analiese described in detail how since that first night, she had continued to suffer bouts of extremely fitful sleep, which usually involved dreams of a disturbing nature. She seemed highly reluctant to elaborate on the qualities of these dreams, although I sensed a degree of embarrassment in her coyness, rather than the fear of being forced to relive her nightmares. At my behest, my colleague took notes while I interviewed the woman, as he later did when we visited others in the area who had been similarly afflicted.

In total we attended the care of four patients, thus infected, in my first week here. I have to say there was a marked degree of similarity in each case. Each of those questioned exhibiting the same lack of vigour, and pallid complexion. They are also, as one, reluctant to elaborate on the nature of their dreams that accompany this illness.

Earlier this week, on the morning that Analiese; dressed in a pale blue dress, with yellow stitching bordering the hems, was laid to rest, we attended the bedside of a young peasant girl named Katharina Bohm. A very sad case indeed given that the child was aged just sixteen years, even more so insofar as her father had raised her alone, the child's mother dying of fever some twelve years earlier.

Her papa, although reluctant to leave his sick child, had gained some work within the forest, and so had not returned home until after dark the previous night. Upon approaching their dwelling, the father heard his daughter moaning and calling out. Believing her to be in pain he strode out to their cottage, only to find upon entering, a most despicable sight. Something dark was astride the girl, its head buried into her chest. According to the peasant, his daughter was indeed crying out, though not as he had first thought in pain, but rather in a way more akin to a couple alone.

Upon his entrance the beast withdrew from the girl, snarling and spitting as it did so. It became apparent that the fiend was a woman, at least of sorts. The black cloak that covered it fell open, to reveal a naked female body, although the things face was twisted into a visage more suited to a demon escaped from hell. The riding-hood seemed to move as though possessed of a life its own, shimmering and distorting as the she-fiend leapt from the bed. The peasant thought his life was done, but instead the creature, now on all fours, bounded past him, moving he thought with an element of gracefulness, like some gigantic cat. Turning back to his daughter, he was distraught to find her nightgown hoisted high around her waist, and the upper fastenings loosed and pulled down, exposing her naked breasts. He covered the girl, and then attempted to wake her, but she never once again opened her eyes. Katharina died in the early hours of yesterday morning.

In this correspondence to you, I shall include copies of all notes taken, and also medical assessments carried out by my colleague and I, in the hope that these things will help to illuminate an answer to this most grave matter. I have only ever read accounts of creatures such as the oupire, and succubus, hence I have no way of truly knowing if such demons can walk among us. Although as you will have reasoned from my contacting you; I do consider this to be a likely explanation. Time is most certainly pressed in dealing with this situation, and I fear that without your expert guidance we may truly be lost. Therefore, I would beseech you to advise me forthwith as to how we may best proceed, in order that we are swiftly able to vanquish this onset of evil.

Sincerely yours,

Doctor Sebastian Alvinci.

Notes to the Reader

Firstly, let me begin by thanking you for having taken the time to read this revised and updated version of *The Cthulhu Child.* I am sure you will agree it is an eclectic selection of short stories. It might be argued, and with some validity, that not all of the stories in this book should be categorized within the horror genre.

However, my original idea when putting this collection together was to demonstrate the true diversity of the term *horror.* Some may regard masked killers, fanged monsters, or demonic entities stalking the night, as the staples of their horror diet. Others prefer the thrills and chills of reading about a Haunted house, or a mysterious cabin in the woods. There are other horrors too. Stories of domestic abuse, social hardship, and even mental illness; any of these can present a basis for more *real world* horrors.

Every Single Night was written as, although prior to the untimely passing of *James Herbert,* a man who was without doubt the Godfather of British horror, and of course it gives a gentle nod of affection to one of his earliest and greatest works, *The Rats.*

If you have never read *The Rats,* then do yourself a favor and purchase a copy today.

Sweet Sugar is a story which means a lot to me. Some may question the validity of placing it in a collection of horror stories, but personal experience has brought me into contact with Dementia and Alzheimer's disease. They are terrible illnesses, and to watch a loved one battle with these conditions is both soul destroying and horrific. My deepest sympathies, and best wishes, go out to all of those who have been touched by this awful affliction. I hope readers with experience of this illness will understand my reasons for including *Sweet Sugar* within these pages.

Losing Him was written in the summer of 2002. A female friend was going through a rather painful break-up, and it is fair to say I drew on aspects of her situation in my writing. Thankfully, she didn't choose to take such a drastic course of action as my story's narrator.

The Cthulhu Child is a story which came about purely by chance. Usually, when I start writing I already have a plot outline running through my head, but this was one occasion where I was a blank slate. I was stuck for ideas, and so decided to put someone behind the wheel of a car, send them on their way, and see what happened next. Actually, I really enjoyed writing this story, and I hope you too enjoyed where their journey took them.

Aphrodite Tears and *Kingdom Falls* are stories which I felt warranted inclusion in this revised edition. *Aphrodite Tears* is a story inclined towards making male readers wince. As with the earlier *Sweet Sugar,* it could be argued that *Kingdom Falls* doesn't technically qualify as horror. It's a matter of personal opinion.

Either way, it is certainly an unsettling little tale.

If you enjoyed the preview to *Carmilla: The Wolves of Styria,* then I hope you will read it in its entirety. It is a novel length reworking of the original tale, and introduces new characters and plots, whilst remaining true to its Gothic roots.

Once again, I thank you for taking the time to read (and hopefully take pleasure from) my work. Any feedback is always appreciated. Please turn the page for details on where to check out my other projects.

Best wishes – David Brian.

http://www.davidbrianwriting.co.uk/

http://www.amazon.co.uk/David-Brian/e/B005OKXVVG/ref=ntt_athr_dp_pel_pop_1

http://www.goodreads.com/author/show/1068132.David_Brian

Printed in Great Britain
by Amazon.co.uk, Ltd.,
Marston Gate.